C0-BGG-393

CLASSIC
StoryTellers

KATHERINE PATERSON

South Huntington Pub. Lib.
145 Pidgeon Hill Rd.
Huntington Sta., N.Y. 11746

Mitchell Lane
PUBLISHERS

P.O. Box 196
Hockessin, Delaware 19707

Titles in the Series

Judy Blume

Ray Bradbury

Beverly Cleary

Stephen Crane

F. Scott Fitzgerald

Nathaniel Hawthorne

Ernest Hemingway

Jack London

Katherine Paterson

Edgar Allan Poe

John Steinbeck

Harriett Beecher Stowe

Mildred Taylor

Mark Twain

E.B. White

CLASSIC
StoryTellers

KATHERINE PATERSON

by Marylou Morano Kjelle

Mitchell Lane PUBLISHERS

Copyright © 2005 by Mitchell Lane Publishers, Inc. All rights reserved. No part of this book may be reproduced without written permission from the publisher. Printed and bound in the United States of America.

Printing 2 3 4 5 6 7 8
   Library of Congress Cataloging-in-Publication Data
Kjelle, Marylou Morano.
      Katherine Paterson / Marylou Kjelle.
         p. cm. — (Classic storytellers)
   Includes bibliographical references and index.
   Contents: A gate of hope — "Spook baby"— A lonely heart— The writer emerges — An honored author.
   ISBN 1-58415-268-0 (lib bdg.)
   1. Paterson, Katherine—Juvenile literature. 2. Authors, American—20th century—Biography—Juvenile literature. 3. Children's stories—Authorship—Juvenile literature. [1. Paterson, Katherine. 2. Authors, American. 3. Women—Biography. 4. Authorship.] I. Title. II. Series.
   PS3566.A779Z75 2004
    813'.54—dc22
                                                                    2003024137
   ISBN 13: 9781584152682

ABOUT THE AUTHOR: Marylou Morano Kjelle is a freelance writer and photojournalist who lives and works in central New Jersey. She is a regular contributor to several local newspapers and online publications. Marylou writes a column for the *Westfield Leader/Times of Scotch Plains—Fanwood* called "Children's Book Nook," where she reviews children's books. She has written twelve nonfiction books for young readers and has an M.S. degree in Science from Rutgers University.

PHOTO CREDITS: Cover, pp. 1, 3, 6 Samantha Loomis Paterson; p. 12, 18, 26, 36 Getty Images; p. 38 Corbis

PUBLISHER'S NOTE: This story is based on the author's extensive research, which she believes to be accurate. Documentation of such research is contained on page 45. While every possible effort has been made to ensure accuracy, the publisher will not assume liability for damages caused by inaccuracies in the data, and makes no warranty on the accuracy of the information contained herein. This story has not been authorized nor endorsed by Katherine Paterson.

The internet sites referenced herein were active as of the publication date. Due to the fleeting nature of some web sites, we cannot guarantee they will all be active when you are reading this book.   PLB2,4

Contents

KATHERINE PATERSON
by Marylou Morano Kjelle

Chapter 1	A Gate of Hope 7
	FYInfo*: The Newbery Medal............................. 11
Chapter 2	"Spook Baby".................. 13
	FYInfo: Manchuria 17
Chapter 3	A Lonely Heart 19
	FYInfo: World War II 25
Chapter 4	The Writer Emerges 27
	FYInfo: Pearl S. Buck 35
Chapter 5	An Honored Author 37
	FYInfo: Flannery O'Connor 42

Chronology 43
Timeline in History 44
Further Reading 45
    For Young Adults 45
    Works Consulted 45
    On The Internet 45
Chapter Notes 46
Glossary 47
Index 48

*For Your Information

Children's author Katherine Paterson is the winner of many awards for her writing, and is one of the very few people to receive two Newbery Medals.

Chapter 1

A GATE OF HOPE

Katherine Paterson's son David was going through a hard time. His small elementary school in Takoma Park, Maryland had closed recently. His new school was much larger and David, a second grader, felt as if he were surrounded by strangers.

As Katherine noted, "at the little school he had been something of the first grade celebrity. Even then he was a natural mimic and very funny little fellow as well as the class artist—famous for his hilarious illustrations."[1]

His new schoolmates treated him in a completely different way. "When he tried to be funny, they thought he was weird; when he drew his comic pictures, they sneered. He came home in tears,"[2] Katherine continued.

Not surprisingly, David was completely miserable. He hated school. Everyday he begged his parents to let him stay home.

Then one day, everything changed. "The funny, happy little boy that I thought I'd lost forever came

Chapter 1 A GATE OF HOPE

running in from school. 'Me and Lisa Hill are making a diorama of Little House in the Big Woods!' he cried, beaming all over. I'd never heard of Lisa Hill until that moment. From then on I was to hear hardly any other name."[3]

David and Lisa became the best of friends. They had a lot of things in common. They both liked art and animals, sports and nature. They played games together. They laughed at each other's jokes. For the rest of the year, David enjoyed school. He and Lisa looked forward to being third graders together after summer vacation was over.

Then one day in August, Katherine answered the phone. She was horrified at the news. Lisa had been struck by lightning. She was dead.

While the entire Paterson family mourned her loss, David was devastated. In his grief, David claimed that God had killed Lisa to punish him. He believed God was going to take everyone he loved, including his mother. He had good reason to be afraid that he might lose his mother. She had recently been diagnosed with cancer. Fortunately, it was detected in the early stages and she was able to recover.

A few months after Lisa's death, Katherine—who had recently published two children's novels—was attending a meeting of writers and publishers in Washington, D.C. Without warning, all her grief and anguish came pouring out as she related the story of David and Lisa's friendship and Lisa's sudden death. The guest of honor, an editor from New York, gently encouraged her to write a story based on what had happened. The thought horrified Katherine. She had used personal experience as the foundation for many of her stories. But this was too personal.

"I thought I couldn't write it, that I was too close and too overwhelmed, but I began to try to write,"[4] Katherine said.

She began by penciling her thoughts in a spiral notebook. From a few random jottings, 32 pages emerged. Katherine moved to her typewriter. For a while, the story progressed relatively smoothly. Then she began encountering problems.

"I [found] myself growing colder with every page until I was totally frozen," she explained later. "The time had come for my fictional child to die, and I could not let it happen."[5]

Katherine found excuses to stay away from her typewriter. She wrote letters. She did loads of laundry. She changed the way that her books were arranged on their shelves. She did housework—lots of housework.

She was on her hands and knees one day, scrubbing her floors in her continuing effort to avoid dealing with her problem. A friend dropped in and asked her how the book was coming along. Katherine explained what happened next.

"I blurted out—'I'm writing a book in which a child dies, and I can't let her die. I guess,' I said, 'I can't face going through Lisa's death again.'

"'Katherine,' she said, looking me in the eye, for she is a true friend, 'I don't think it's Lisa's death you can't face. I think it's yours.'"[6]

That was the spark that Katherine—recovering from her cancer but still anxious about it—needed.

"I went straight home to my study and closed the door," she continued. "If it was my death I could not face, then by God, I would face it. I began in a kind of fever, and in a day I had written the chapter, and within a few weeks I had completed the draft, the cold sweat pouring down my arms."[7]

Normally, completing the first draft of a book is just the beginning of a much longer process. Authors almost always spend far more time revising and rewriting before considering that the book is finished and sending it away to publishers. Not this time.

Chapter 1 A GATE OF HOPE

"Because I could not stand to have it around, I did what no real writer would ever do—I mailed the manuscript to my editor," Katherine said. "As soon as I left the post office, I was seized with terror. What had I done? What would my editor think of this terrible book?"[8]

She didn't have to worry. The editor liked what Katherine had written, even though it was not ready to be published. Katherine didn't mind. She has always loved revising her books. This one was no exception. Getting the first draft on paper had been a horrible experience. Preparing it for publication proved to be a pleasure.

Entitled *Bridge to Terabithia*, the book is the story of the friendship of two fifth-graders, Leslie Burke and Jesse Aarons. The two create an imaginary land named Terabithia in the nearby woods. Ultimately one of the characters dies tragically. While the book is fiction, it is based on the friendship between David and Lisa. Katherine dedicated the book to them.

Published in 1977, *Bridge to Terabithia* was awarded the Newbery Medal the following year. The Newbery Medal is the highest honor a children's book can receive in the United States. Since then, *Bridge to Terabithia* has sold millions of copies and has been translated into 25 languages.

When Lisa died, her family had been afraid that no one would ever hear of her or know about her life. Now Lisa's spirit lives on in the hearts and minds of everyone who has read *Bridge to Terabithia*. The book has taught them that friendship can create a bridge. Where there is a bridge, there also lies a gate of hope.

FYInfo

The Newbery Medal

John Newbery, born in England in 1713, is thought to be the first person to publish children's books. At the age of 24 he inherited a printing business. Seven years later, he wrote as well as published *A Little Pretty Pocket Book,* his first book for young readers. This book was an illustrated listing of children's entertainment, based upon the alphabet. Newbery eventually expanded *A Little Pretty Pocket Book* into a series of books for young readers. He was a firm believer in literacy for children and promoted books not only for education, but also for the endless hours of entertainment they could provide.

In addition to writing his own books, Newbery hired writers and illustrators to create children's books. It is believed that the Irish poet and novelist, Oliver Goldsmith, was one of Newbery's children's book writers. Newbery's Juvenile Library consisted of small attractive books containing either single stories or collections. In 1751, Newbery introduced children to magazines when he released *The Lilliputian Magazine,* the first periodical written for children. Newbery was the principal writer of *The Lilliputian Magazine,* which included songs, stories and fairy tales.

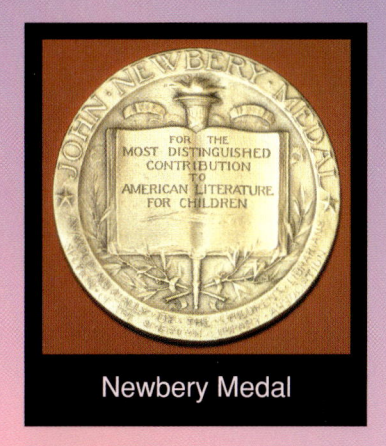

Newbery Medal

After his death in 1767, Newbery's family inherited his publishing house. They carried on his legacy and expanded the number of published children's books to 400.

In 1921, Frederic G. Melcher, the co-editor of *Publishers Weekly* magazine, proposed that the American Library Association institute an annual award to writers of children's literature. Suggesting it be named in honor of John Newbery, Melcher stated the purpose of the award was "to encourage original creative work in the field of books for children."[1]

Since 1922, the American Library Association's Association for Library Service to Children has awarded the Newbery Medal annually to the author of the most distinguished American children's book published the previous year. Several other outstanding titles receive recognition as Newbery Honor Books each year.

Chinese General Chiang Kai-Shek and Communist leader Mao Zedong stand side by side in 1945. The two leaders were enemies until Japan attacked China and they joined forces to fight the invaders.

Chapter 2

"SPOOK BABY"

Katherine Paterson was born on Halloween—October 31—in 1932 in the city of Tsing-Tsing Pu in the Chinese province of Jiangsu. It was a time and place of considerable unrest. In the 1930s, Jiangsu was the site of many battles between the nationalist government headed by Chiang Kai-shek and the Chinese communists led by Mao Zedong.

The story of Katherine's birth in such a tumultuous place at such a tumultuous time begins on the other side of the world in the southern states of the United States. Katherine's mother, Mary Goetchius, hailed from Georgia. Mary's mother was a stern and proper lady whom Katherine feared more than loved. Mary's father's two older brothers died fighting for the South in the Civil War. One was a cavalry officer who was killed in Pickett's Charge at Gettysburg.

Katherine's father, George Raymond Womeldorf, grew up in Lexington in the Shenandoah Valley of Virginia. His family had lived there for many years. Although the Womeldorfs were farmers, they never

Chapter 2   "SPOOK BABY"

owned slaves. Like the famous writer Ernest Hemingway, George volunteered to be an ambulance driver for the French army during World War I. He was wounded by shrapnel and poison gas. Eventually he had to have his right leg amputated.

After he recovered from his war injuries, George attended a seminary—a school for religious studies—so he could become a pastor in the Presbyterian Church. There he met Mary Goetchius. The two had many interests in common. One was the desire to be missionaries and bring Christianity to the Asian people. George and Mary were married in June, 1923. Later that year they sailed to China to begin their service.

Katherine was the Womeldorfs' third child. She joined Raymond, an older brother whom the family called Sonny, and a sister, Lizzie. Sonny and Lizzie often teased Katherine, calling her "Spook Baby" because she was born on Halloween. Two more sisters, Helen and Anne, would complete the family. Sonny and Lizzie got along well, and Helen and Anne had each other. This left Katherine feeling somewhat isolated throughout her childhood.

She spent her very early years in the ancient city of Hwaian (now spelled Huaian) in the eastern section of China. Hwaian sits on the banks of the Grand Canal, the world's oldest and longest artificial waterway at more than 1000 miles. Her father served as the principal for a school for boys. Unlike most foreigners during that era, their neighbors were Chinese. The family lived inside the gates of the school in a pagoda-style house heated by a coal burning stove. The Womeldorf children enjoyed playing in the backyard and riding a special merry-go-round that had been built for them. The family had a nurse, called an *amah*, and a cook who prepared delicious Chinese meals. One of Katherine's favorite foods was steamed pork dumplings. "Katherine, if you keep eating so much Chinese food, you might turn into a little Chinese girl,"[1] her mother teased.

There was a bit of truth behind the teasing. Although her hair was blond and curly, Katherine considered herself Chinese, not American. At home, Katherine spoke English, but she spoke Chinese to her neighborhood playmates.

Katherine's father was away from home much of the time during her early years. He and a Christian pastor named Mr. Lee rode donkeys to faraway villages and farms, preaching and delivering food and medicine. Although Katherine missed her father very much when he was away, she kept busy. She visited her neighbor, Mrs. Loo, who would prepare Katherine's favorite foods whenever she dropped in for lunch. There was also school work to complete. Because there were no English schools in China, Katherine's mother taught her children at home.

Katherine's parents valued books and taught her to love them from a very early age. By the time she was five she had taught herself to read.

Mrs. Womeldorf often read to her children. Katherine remembers her favorite books being read over and over again in her mother's soft Southern accent. "I can almost recite from heart the poems and stories of A. A. Milne, and I loved *The Wind in the Willows* almost as fanatically as the youth of the sixties loved Tolkien,"[2] Katherine says. Her favorite books were the Winnie the Pooh books, *The Tale of Peter Rabbit*, *The Jungle Book* and fairy tales by the brothers Grimm and Hans Christian Andersen. Not surprisingly, she also spent a good deal of time reading the Bible.

The peace inside the Womeldorf home was soon shattered. A few months before Katherine's birth, Japan had invaded Manchuria, an industrial province of northeast China. War came much closer in the summer of 1937, when Japan launched a much larger

Chapter 2 — "SPOOK BABY"

invasion. The communists and nationalists stopped fighting each other and joined forces to fight their common enemy.

Night after night, bombs from Japanese airplanes fell around the mountain town of Kuling (now known as Lushan), where the Womeldorfs had gone to escape the heat. Katherine's father had returned to Hwaian to continue his missionary work and see to the school, but the war kept the rest of the family in Kuling. Although the bombings made Katherine long for her home in Hwaian, she attended kindergarten with other missionary children. She found it difficult, but enjoyed singing in the children's choir that formed for the Christmas holidays. Katherine worried about her father. She knew the Chinese countryside was full of opposing armies, outlaws and warlords, and she wanted him to be safe.

In early 1938, the Presbyterian Mission Board asked the Womeldorfs to leave China and return to America for their own safety. The family didn't intend to stay in America permanently. They planned to return to China as soon as it was once again safe to live there.

To travel to America, the family took a train from Kuling to Hong Kong, then boarded a German ship to Southampton, England. Katherine noticed a picture of a stern-looking man with a stubby black mustache hanging on the walls of the ship. The man was Adolf Hitler, the dictator of Germany. In Southampton, Katherine's family boarded another ship which took them across the Atlantic Ocean to New York. Katherine was about to be introduced to her home country.

FYInfo

Manchuria

Manchuria is a largely mountainous area in northeastern China. Rivers form its borders with Russia to the north and east and North Korea to the south, while a range of mountains separates it from Mongolia in the west. Food crops, cotton, wool and tobacco grow in Manchuria's fertile valleys. Manchuria is also known for its silk industry and its underground reserves of coal, minerals and iron ore.

Manchuria's rich natural resources and its strategic location have been natural magnets for countries that want to control it, particularly Russia and Japan. Japan conquered part of Manchuria in 1895, but Russia, Germany and France were concerned about Japan's growing power and forced the Japanese to withdraw. As a result, Russia controlled Manchuria from 1898 to 1904. After defeating Russia in the Russo-Japanese War in 1905, Japan seized the southern part of Manchuria. For more than a decade after World War I, Chinese warlords controlled most of Manchuria's territory.

The Chinese Civil War, which began in the late 1920s, exhausted China's military might. That made it easy for the Japanese to invade Manchuria in 1931. Japan's takeover of Manchuria was equal to a declaration of war against China. Japan changed Manchuria's name to Manchukuo and made it a supposedly independent state, though the Japanese were really in control. Manchukuo served Japan well during World War II as the region supplied metals, coal, petroleum and chemicals for Japan's war effort. During the last days of World War II, the Soviet Union—which had been formed in 1922 under Russia's leadership—declared war on Japan and occupied Manchuria.

After the war, the Soviet Union helped the Chinese Communists use Manchuria as a staging base for their conflict with the nationalist government. This greatly helped the Communists to conquer all of China by 1949. During the 1960s, China claimed some Soviet territory beyond Manchuria. In 1969, China and the Soviet Union clashed over control of several islands in one of the rivers that divided the two countries. The fighting stopped after the two nations agreed to discuss their differences. The border issue was settled when the Soviet Union broke up in 1991.

Manchuria

A barge in a canal in Shanghai as it looks today. Katherine Paterson was born in the nearby province of Jiangsu in 1932.

Chapter 3

A LONELY HEART

While Katherine's parents traveled around the country talking about their experiences in China, their children stayed on the same farm in Lexington, Virginia where their father had lived as a boy. Because Katherine had only known life in China, the United States felt like a foreign country to her. She missed her parents and her home in Hwaian. She missed Mr. Lee and Mrs. Loo and her wonderful steamed dumplings. To deal with her homesickness, Katherine spent much of her time by herself, acting out fantasy stories she read or made up. She portrayed all the different characters, often speaking their lines out loud.

Katherine's vivid imagination stayed with her throughout her childhood. She had the ability to be a storyteller from an early age. Her imagination also helped her deal with her loneliness.

"I spent my early years as an outsider looking in, entertaining myself, doing a lot of reading and writing,"[1] Katherine said.

Late in 1938, Katherine's parents returned from their tour around the country and relocated their

Chapter 3   A LONELY HEART

family to Richmond, Virginia. The school year had already begun, and Katherine was placed in the first grade. It was a difficult period for her, especially because she was too shy to make friends. On Valentine's Day, she cheerfully distributed valentines to all her classmates. She didn't get a single one in return. She managed to hold back her tears until she got home, then cried as if she would never stop. Katherine's mother never forgot that Valentine's Day.

"My mother grieved over this event until her death, asking me once why I didn't write a story about the time I didn't get any valentines," Katherine recalled much later. 'But mother,' I said, 'all my stories are about the time I didn't get any valentines.'"[2]

In 1939 the Womeldorfs were allowed to return to China. It was still too dangerous to return to Hwaian. The family settled in Shanghai, where they lived in the British section. Katherine soon spoke with a British accent. While her father went on trips delivering medicine to missionary hospitals, Katherine attended second grade at Shanghai American School. She appeared in print for the first time, with a poem that was published in the school newspaper, the *Shanghai American*. It went:

Pat! Pat! Pat!
There is the cat.
Where is the rat?
Pat! Pat! Pat!

When summer arrived, Mrs. Womeldorf and the children moved to Qingdao, a beach town on the Yellow Sea. There Katherine spent many long lazy days playing with other missionary children. Other days weren't as peaceful. Japanese soldiers conducted practice invasions on the beach, quite close to the Womeldorfs' house. It was a frightening experience.

"I was out playing and heard this blood-chilling sound," she said. "Soldiers wearing only a loincloth and carrying guns with bayonets were coming up our yard. I grabbed my little sister's hand and ran for all I was worth."[3]

KATHERINE PATERSON

In 1940, her father accepted a position running a hospital in Zhenjiang. Housing was short so the family lived at the hospital, sleeping in one of the rooms normally used by patients. There were no schools in Zhenjiang, so Katherine's mother and another mother taught the missionary children. Many times the lessons were interrupted by Japanese soldiers who came in to question the mothers and their children about their activities.

By December China was no longer safe for missionary families. Again the Womeldorfs set out for America. World War II had been underway for more than a year. Even though the United States had not yet entered the conflict, returning home was dangerous.

The Womeldorfs settled in Lynchburg, Virginia. Katherine became friendly with her cousin, Nancy Spencer. Nancy's father owned a construction company, and the two girls played with cinder blocks and other construction materials stored in the yard.

Katherine really enjoyed school for the first time in third grade. She had good grades, liked her teacher, and was even asked to play the witch in the class play, *Sleeping Beauty*. This happiness did not last long. The following year her father was asked to pastor a church in Winston-Salem, North Carolina, where Katherine entered the Calvin H. Wiley School. She was called the "mish kid" because her parents had been missionaries. Her classmates knew only that she had come from somewhere across the ocean. When the Japanese bombed the U.S. naval base at Pearl Harbor, Hawaii on December 7, 1941, the United States declared war on Japan. Some of Katherine's schoolmates thought Japan and China were the same country. They called her a "Jap" and accused her of being a Japanese spy.

That wasn't her only problem. The many moves Katherine endured as a child—she estimated that she moved 18 times in her first 18 years—were hard on her. Every time the family relocated,

Chapter 3 A LONELY HEART

she became the new kid in school and in the neighborhood. She had difficulty making friends as well as getting along with her classmates. She was shy, spoke with a British accent (which made her stand out) and wore hand-me-down clothes. On more than one occasion, her classmates pointed out that the outfit she was wearing had belonged to them the previous year. Katherine felt lonely and set apart from children her own age.

Katherine draws upon those lonely years when writing her books. "It's very easy for me to identify with a child who's on the outside, but the thing I think I have learned since I've grown up is that almost everybody feels as though he or she is on the outside. When you write about an outsider you're not writing about just a few exceptions, you're writing about most of the world,"[4] she said.

The one place Katherine felt at home was the school library. She became a library aide. One of her responsibilities was to read aloud to younger children. Another was mending the bindings on older books. To Katherine, however, the library was more than a job. It was a place where she could read. One of her most cherished books was Frances Hodgson Burnett's *The Secret Garden*. A character in the book, Mary Lennox, lives in different places. Katherine could relate to Mary's situation. *The Secret Garden* is a story of hope, and it gave Katherine a reason to believe that her life would get better in time.

Books transported Katherine out of Calvin H. Wiley School, where she was an outsider. They transported her to her own special world where her abilities were endless. Katherine could not get enough of books. She read at night with a flashlight under her bed covers. The first book she could truly call her own was the Pulitzer Prize-winning *The Yearling*, by Marjorie Kinnan Rawlings. Once again Katherine related to the book's main character, a young Southern boy named Jody who often feels alone and out of place. Jody deals with his loneliness by keeping a deer as a pet.

Slowly she emerged from her isolation. By fifth grade, Katherine had become well-liked by her schoolmates, who looked forward to performing in the plays and skits that she wrote. She was no longer considered different or strange—or a spy! She was even elected student body president.

Katherine's new popularity did not cause her to abandon her love of books. Once she came home from school with a copy of Charles Dickens' book about the French Revolution, *A Tale of Two Cities*. Without removing her overcoat, she fell on the floor and read until supper time. Katherine's mother swept the rug around her, but Katherine's grandmother reprimanded her and called her a "lover of luxury."[5]

Another book that influenced Katherine was Alan Paton's *Cry, the Beloved Country*, a book about South Africa. "*Cry, the Beloved Country* was a pivotal book for me," Katherine wrote. "On reading it I had to face myself in a way I never had before. It was this book more than any other that enabled me to discover myself. [My discovery] made a kind of healing and growth possible. A great book can do this for a reader. It can give us hope as it judges us."[6]

Yet for all her love of books and reading, and for all the writing she did as a child, the thought that she might become a writer did not occur to Katherine. Her life's plan was to become an actress and a movie star.

World War II came to an end in 1945. The Womeldorfs began making arrangements to return to China. Mr. Womeldorf resigned his position as the pastor of the Winston-Salem church and once again worked for the Presbyterian Missionary Board. Katherine was the oldest of the three children who would return with their parents to China. Sonny was in the U.S. Navy and Lizzie was planning to attend college.

Chapter 3   A LONELY HEART

The wait to return to China went on and on. One day, without meaning to, Katherine read a letter that the missionary board had sent to her father. The board believed that she was too old to accompany her parents to China. They suggested that she stay behind and attend a boarding school.

Katherine knew how much her parents wanted to depart for China. Now that she knew she was the cause of the delay, she confronted them with her newfound information and urged them to return without her. They refused to leave her behind.

Katherine completed her freshman and sophomore years of high school in Richmond. By now it was evident that the Womeldorfs were not returning to China. The family moved yet again, this time to a small West Virginia town called Charles Town. Katherine's experience might have been difficult. All the students had known each other for years and could have resented an outsider. Fortunately, they quickly invited Katherine to join them in their activities. Katherine continued her acting at Charles Town High School. Some of the productions Katherine starred in went on to win state awards.

By the time she graduated from high school in 1950, Katherine had put aside her dream of becoming a movie star. She decided to follow in her parents' footsteps and become a missionary. She received a scholarship to attend King College, a small liberal arts college located near the Great Smoky Mountains in Bristol, Tennessee. Her goal was to become a teacher, teach for a year to gain some experience, then attend graduate school and study to become a missionary—preferably in China. She had no idea that her life would take an almost completely different direction.

FYInfo

World War II

Throughout the 1930s, Germany, under the dictatorship of Adolf Hitler, started to test the limits of the treaties it had agreed to following the surrender that brought World War I to a conclusion. After building up their armed forces, the Germans annexed Austria early in 1938. Soon afterward, Germany took over Czechoslovakia. England and France, concerned about starting another World War, allowed Hitler's aggression. But when Germany invaded Poland in September 1939, the two countries declared war on Germany. World War II had begun.

Before invading Poland, Germany signed a non-aggression treaty with Russia. As the war progressed, Italy and Japan entered the war on Germany's side. These three nations called themselves the "Axis Powers." Less than a year after the invasion of Poland, most of the remaining European countries, including France, had fallen to the Germans. Though the United States had not yet entered the war, President Franklin Roosevelt provided England with American supplies. Under the leadership of Prime Minister Winston Churchill, England fought the Axis powers on two fronts: North Africa as well as Europe.

The Japanese bombing of Pearl Harbor on December 7, 1941, brought the United States into the war. By that time, Germany had broken its non-aggression pact with Russia and was fighting on Russian soil. Russia joined the Allies, the countries fighting Germany and Japan. The American victory at the Battle of Midway in June 1942 halted Japanese expansion in the Pacific. Early the following year, the Russians stopped the German advance at the Battle of Stalingrad. On D-Day—June 6, 1944—American, British and Canadian troops landed on the French coast of Normandy and began to drive the Germans out of France. At the same time, the Russian army marched towards the German capital of Berlin. Less than a year later Germany surrendered. In August 1945, the United States dropped two atomic bombs on Japan. A few weeks later, the long war was finally over. Fifty-five million people—both civilian and military—were killed during World War II.

Winston Churchill

Gerard Manley Hopkins was a Jesuit priest and Victorian poet who lived from 1844-1889. Hopkins was the inspiration for Paterson's main character in The Great Gilly Hopkins.

Chapter 4

THE WRITER EMERGES

Katherine was happy during her four years at King College. It was the longest she had lived in one place since she was a small child. She took part in theatrical productions and sang in the school chorus. She majored in English, and studied classical writers like Emily Dickinson and William Shakespeare. She was also introduced to the poetry of Gerard Manley Hopkins. Years later Katherine would use Hopkins' name in the title of one of her books.

Katherine graduated summa cum laude (with high honors). She became a sixth grade teacher in Lovettsville, Virginia, a poor community situated in Virginia's beautiful Blue Ridge Mountains. The conditions under which she taught were not as attractive. The school had no library or lunchroom. Her classroom was located in the school's basement. It was packed with 36 students. Some were as old as 16 because they had failed several grades over the years.

Fortunately, her students were polite and respectful. It was difficult for them to imagine a world be-

Chapter 4   THE WRITER EMERGES

yond the mountains that enclosed them, so they loved hearing about Katherine's experiences in China. Katherine did her best to instill optimism into her class. She brought her own books to school and read them aloud. She took her students on a field trip to Washington D.C.

While Katherine enjoyed teaching, she was sometimes lonely for her family and friends. To bolster her spirits, each morning she would tell herself that something wonderful would happen sometime during the day. She learned to find joy in simple things, such as reading a good book or an academic achievement of one of her students. The school year passed quickly and happily. Although her future missionary work would take Katherine to places far from Lovettsville, the year she spent in the school basement was never far from her heart. She modeled Lark Creek Elementary School in *Bridge to Terabithia* after the school in Lovettsville.

In 1957, according to plan, Katherine earned a masters degree at the Presbyterian School of Christian Education in Richmond, Virginia. In addition to obtaining her degree, two very important things happened to Katherine while she was at the school. One was a conversation with one of her professors, Sara Little, who asked Katherine if she had ever thought of pursuing a career as a writer. Katherine expressed doubts at her ability. She was afraid of failure and didn't want to write unless she was sure she could be excellent at it.

"Maybe that's what God is calling you to be,"[1] Sara responded.

With the help of her professor, Katherine came to realize that if she wasn't willing to risk not being the best at what ever she did, she wouldn't do anything at all. While she didn't immediately become a writer, the conversation helped to make her ready when an opportunity to write came along several years later.

KATHERINE PATERSON

The other important event came when she found out that she couldn't return to China as a missionary as she had hoped. The communists had taken over the government of China and were not allowing Westerners into the country. Her parents had encountered the same problem. Eventually foreigners were allowed back into China, but by then, Mr. Womeldorf had lost his desire to return. The communists had killed his good friend, Mr. Lee, and he was heartbroken.

While she was deciding what to do, Katherine met Ai, a female pastor from Japan. Since Katherine couldn't go to China, Ai encouraged her to become a missionary in Japan instead. It was a difficult decision for Katherine to make. She had bitter memories of the Japanese because she remembered them as the enemies who had brutally invaded her beloved China. Ai convinced Katherine to give Japan a chance, and in the summer of 1957, Katherine departed. She would spend two years learning the Japanese language and two years as a missionary.

Learning the Japanese language was more difficult than Katherine had anticipated. She also had to become accustomed to the traditions and rituals of the Japanese people, such as learning to sleep on a mat on the floor. After completing her language studies, Katherine lived in a fishing village in Shikoku, the smallest of Japan's four main islands. Her home was owned by members of a Buddhist sect that was strongly anti-Christian. At times it was difficult for Katherine, who had come to Japan to preach the Christian religion, to listen to her landlords chant their Buddhist prayers.

Katherine used a small motor bike to travel around the island. She went from church to church, preaching and helping eleven pastors teach Christian education. All the while, Katherine continued to work on improving her Japanese pronunciation by studying privately with a tutor. Before long she was preaching in

Chapter 4   THE WRITER EMERGES

both English and Japanese. By then her attitude toward Japan had completely changed.

"In the course of four years I was set fully free from my deep childish hatred," Katherine said. "I truly loved Japan, and one of the most heart-warming compliments I ever received came from a Japanese man I worked with who said to me one day that someone had told him that I had been born in China. Was that true? I assured him it was. 'I knew it,' he said. 'I've always known there was something Oriental about you.'"[2]

When her four years in Japan were up, the missionary board required Katherine to return to the United States for a one-year period. She had every intention of going back to Japan.

As much as she missed her family while she had been in Japan, it was difficult to be home. Now 28 years old, she had become an independent, self-assured young woman during the course of her missionary work. The Katherine who had left the United States for Japan was not the same young woman who returned. Once again she felt like an outsider. This time she was isolated from her own family.

"The reason I thought my family didn't know me was that they didn't know me in Japanese," she explains. "In those four years I had become a different person. I had not only learned new ways to express myself, I had new thoughts to express."[3]

While she waited for the year to pass, she enrolled in Union Theological Seminary in New York City to study for a second master's degree. There she met John Barstow Paterson, a young minister from Buffalo, New York. He took an immediate liking to Katherine. At first Katherine was unsure of her feelings towards him, though she soon came to realize that she loved him. They were married on July 14, 1962. Katherine did not return to Japan as she had planned. Instead, she moved to Buffalo so John could continue to serve his church.

KATHERINE PATERSON

The following year, Katherine and John moved to Princeton, New Jersey, where John studied at the seminary at Princeton University. Katherine taught sacred studies at Pennington School, a private school for boys. The Patersons' first child, John Paterson, Jr., was born in 1964. Katherine and John hoped to have four children—two of their own (or "homemade" as Katherine often refers to them) and two adopted. When John Jr. was six months old, the Patersons became the parents of a two-year-old girl from an orphanage in Hong Kong, China. They named her Elizabeth PoLin and called her Lin for short.

At about the same time, Katherine received a request that would change her life. The Presbyterian Board of Christian Education asked her to write a book for middle grade readers that could be used in the church school curriculum. The idea intrigued Katherine. She felt the project would allow her to combine her degree in Christian Education with the love of stories she had nourished since she was a child. She may have also recalled professor Sara Little's challenging words. Working in brief increments around the demands of her household, Katherine completed her first book, *Who Am I?* It is a book of encouragement that teaches as well as inspires young readers to explore different aspects of religion.

In 1965, the Patersons moved to Takoma Park, located outside of Washington, D.C. John became pastor of the Takoma Park Presbyterian Church. Later that same year, Katherine gave birth to their second son, David. Two years later, they adopted five-month-old Mary Katherine Nah-he-sa-pe-che-a, an Apache-Kiowa baby.

Soon after moving to Takoma Park, Katherine joined a creative writing class. She tried different types of writing and discovered that she enjoyed fiction the most. While having four children under the age of five kept her extremely busy, writing soon

Chapter 4 THE WRITER EMERGES

became an important a part of her life. She wrote stories for adults and submitted them to magazines in whatever small scraps of time she could find for the next seven years—with almost nothing to show for all her efforts. She collected scores of rejection slips with only two small sales. One was a short story published by a Roman Catholic magazine that went out of business shortly thereafter. The other was a poem. The magazine that bought it folded before her poem could even be published.

With John's encouragement, Katherine kept writing. She admits that not much of what she wrote during this time was really good. "I was learning how to write," she says, "and I am glad that most of that writing still sits in my drawer rather than out in public for people to see."[4]

Around this time, Katherine started a tradition at Takoma Park Presbyterian Church. She wrote Christmas stories that were read at the yearly Christmas Eve service. These stories were eventually collected into a book titled *Angels and Other Strangers* and published in 1979.

Because of the difficulty that Katherine was having in getting her adult writing published, she took a class in children's writing. That encouraged her to write a story with a Japanese setting. The idea for the plot came from Lin, who was five at the time and struggling with her abandonment by her birth mother. Katherine decided to write a book about a young boy searching for his father in feudal Japan. The book consumed many hours of research, writing and re-writing. Then she began sending it out to publishers.

Again she experienced the discouragement of rejection slips. For two years, publisher after publisher turned it down. Finally Crowell Publishers accepted it. Entitled *The Sign of the Chrysanthemum*, the book was published in 1973.

The idea for Katherine's second novel, *Of Nightingales That Weep*, came from a friend who asked her to write a book with a strong female character. As Katherine began writing about her book's heroine, Takiko, other traits began to emerge. Takiko was vain and selfish. The heroine Katherine started out to write turned into an entirely new person. Katherine believed that Takiko would be more believable this way. A person without any faults wouldn't be very convincing.

Katherine's next book came in response to her children's request that she create a mystery story. Katherine was hesitant. "I like mysteries," she told her children, "but it takes a certain kind of brain to write them, and I don't have that kind of brain. I haven't been able to beat Lin at chess since she was six."[5]

Instead of writing a straight mystery, Katherine thought she would write an adventure story that contained a lot of suspense. Soon afterward, she got the idea for what would become *The Master Puppeteer* when she saw a photograph of a Japanese warrior puppet in a newspaper. The puppet was part of Bunraku, classical Japanese puppet theatre that Katherine had attended and enjoyed when she was living in Japan. She thought that a puppet theatre would be the perfect setting for her story, which would take place in the late 18th century.

Katherine was further convinced that she had to write the story when she dreamed about a young boy searching for something on the second floor of an old Japanese warehouse. What was the boy searching for, and what part could the searching play in her new book?

Katherine felt that to write the best book possible about Bunraku, she needed to travel to Japan to complete her research. John encouraged her to contact her publisher and ask to have her advance—the money an author receives before a book is placed in

Chapter 4 THE WRITER EMERGES

bookstores and sold—doubled. The publisher agreed. Katherine and Lin, now ten years old, set off for Japan.

The trip was productive. Katherine attended Bunraku performances and interviewed puppeteers. She also studied what life was like in the late 1700s, and the experiences that people living during that time would have had.

With her research complete, Katherine and Lin had one more stop to make before they returned home. Lin had always wanted to know about her birth mother and the orphanage where she had spent the first two years of her life. She wondered why her birth mother hadn't kept her. Katherine and Lin went to Hong Kong and visited the orphanage. The visit did not reveal much to Lin about her past. It did reveal where her future lay—with the Patersons.

When Katherine began to work on her new book, she encountered something feared by all writers: writer's block. Katherine tried hard to write the story, but the words would not come. Although it was a struggle, Katherine forced herself to sit at her typewriter every day until she had completed a first draft. She was so unhappy with the result that she came close to destroying her manuscript.

It was a good thing she didn't. After her frightening experience with cancer and her recovery, she finished revising *The Master Puppeteer*. It was published in 1976. The following year, she won the National Book Award in Children's Literature for the book. Some people immediately said that she was an overnight success. Katherine laughed at those comments. She knew that the so-called night had actually lasted for nine years. The National Book Award was her first major honor. It would hardly be the last.

FYInfo

Pearl S. Buck

The early life of Nobel Prize-winning author Pearl S. Buck closely resembles that of Katherine Paterson. Pearl was born in 1892 in Hillsboro, West Virginia. Like Katherine, she spent her early years in China. Pearl's parents were also Presbyterian missionaries. Like Katherine's family, Pearl and her family lived side by side with the Chinese people, not in isolated missionary neighborhoods. Although she was blond and blue-eyed, Pearl considered herself Chinese and not American. She spoke the Chinese language and grew to love the Chinese culture.

In 1910, Pearl returned to the United States to attend Randolph-Macon Women's College in Lynchburg, Virginia. After graduating, Pearl returned to China. Soon she met and married John Lossing Buck. The two of them worked as teachers at a missionary school for Chinese boys. While in China, she wrote articles on the Chinese people and culture that were published in American magazines. In 1931, Pearl's novel, *The Good Earth*, the story of a Chinese peasant's relationship to his land and people, was published. In 1932, it received the Pulitzer Prize for Literature. After receiving her award, Pearl relocated to Pennsylvania, divorced her husband and married her publisher, Richard Walsh. She and her new husband adopted six children. She continued to write and in 1938 received the Nobel Prize for Literature. She was the first American woman to win this prestigious award.

Pearl was a compassionate person who used her writing to bring social issues to the forefront. She was an advocate for civil rights and mentally retarded children (Pearl had a daughter who was retarded). She also supported adoption, especially of mixed-race children, and started her own adoption agency to insure that all children had an equal chance at finding a loving home. In her later years she advised President Richard Nixon on Chinese-American relations. This earned her the title of "Woman of Two Worlds." In 1973, Pearl Buck died of cancer in Vermont. Her many books, articles and stories continue to bridge the gap between two countries and help people of two cultures understand each other. It can be said that Katherine Paterson's books do the same.

The USS John F. Kennedy docks at Naval Station Norfolk near Norfolk, Virginia. In 1977 the Patersons moved to Norfolk where Katherine's husband, John became pastor of Lafayette Presbyterian Church.

Chapter 5

AN HONORED AUTHOR

In 1977, the Patersons moved to Norfolk, Virginia, where John became pastor of Lafayette Presbyterian Church. *Bridge to Terabithia* was published that same year, and won the Newbery Medal in 1978.

Katherine was just getting started. Her next book, *The Great Gilly Hopkins*, showed how she could take an unhappy personal experience and turn it into a book that would appeal to young readers.

"I wrote Gilly after I'd been a foster mother for a couple of months and didn't feel as though I'd been such a great one, so I tried to imagine how it might be to be a foster child," she explained. How would I feel if I thought the rest of the world thought of me as disposable?"[1]

It was named a Newbery Honor Book in 1979. Two years later, *Jacob Have I Loved* won a second Newbery Medal for Katherine. That put her among the handful of multiple Newbery Medal winners. She is only just one of two (Richard Peck is the other) to win the coveted award twice within a three-year period.

Chapter 5 AN HONORED AUTHOR

These awards meant that within a decade after the publication of *The Sign of the Chrysanthemum*, her first children's novel, Katherine had become a major figure in children's literature. She would go on to win many other honors. Among them are the Scott O'Dell Award, the National Book Award for Children's Literature, the American Book Award, the American Library Association's Best Books for Young Adults Award, the New York Times Outstanding Books of the Year Award, the School Library Journal Best Books Award, the Children's Book Council's Children's Choice Award, and the Edgar Allan Poe Award.

Hans Christian Andersen (1805-1875) was a Danish author, best known for his fairy tales. An author's award, named in his honor, which recognizes internationally-known authors, has been given since 1956. In 1998 it was given to Katherine Paterson.

What is perhaps her highest honor came in 1998 when she became just the fifth American to win the Hans Christian Andersen Award. This award is sometimes called the "Little Nobel Prize," after the famous annual awards in fields such as literature, medicine and science. It is the highest international award in children's literature, and recognizes an author's entire body of work.

Katherine's body of work now includes more than 30 books which have been translated into many languages. In the course of writing these books, Katherine has created many memorable characters that she gets to know intimately. Just as if they were real people, she feels for their pain. It hurts her when something terrible happens to them, but she knows that her characters must experience difficulties for her readers to receive something valuable from her writing. In all her writing, Katherine hopes that children identify with her characters and that they will "come to love and forgive the people on the page to be able to forgive and love their own deepest selves."[2]

For all the honors and esteem that Katherine's books have garnered, there have been people who have been critical of them. Because of its profanity, hints of sexuality, disrespect to adults, references to magic and praying to spirits, *Bridge to Terabithia* often appears on lists of the ten books whose inclusion in schools and libraries is most frequently challenged. Ironically, in view of her strong religious roots, many of these attacks have come from Christian groups.

That's not all. There are complaints that her characters aren't likeable. Some people have called her books depressing. Additional objections have come from literary critics, who have faulted Katherine for writing each of her books in a different style.

Chapter 5 AN HONORED AUTHOR

Katherine might reply that it is the opinions of her young readers that she values most. Typical is what one boy wrote in a book report about *The Great Gilly Hopkins*: "This book is a miracle. Mrs. Paterson knows exactly how children feel."[3]

In addition, she draws on the firm foundation of her Presbyterian background and regards her ability to write as a God-given gift. To honor that gift, she believes that she must write from her heart, not according to the guidelines that others might try to set for her. She believes that her stories all have an inevitable ending. If she tries to write another ending, she will not be doing the right thing for her story, and her readers will recognize it. As a result, many of her stories include unpleasant experiences. Some end unhappily, though that does not mean that they end in despair.

"I cannot, will not, withhold from my young readers the harsh realities of human hunger and suffering and loss, but neither will I neglect to plant that stubborn seed of hope that has enabled our race to outlast wars and famines and the destruction of death,"[4] she said.

Her beliefs also help her deal with her stylistic critics. "I really don't even think about style," she said. "I think about the story. And it seems to me the story demands its own style. Just as the ending is not something I can manipulate, so is the style. And I think one of the hard things about writing a book is discovering the style of the book, the language that history demands to be written in. In other words, discovering the proper voice, the right rhythm and the music of that particular book."[5]

Katherine's personal rhythm has become very different as she has grown older. After moving so frequently when she was young, and several more times following her marriage, she was finally able to settle into one place. In 1986, John became the pastor of the First Presbyterian Church in Barre, Vermont. The Patersons have remained there ever since.

During their years in Barre, Katherine and John have collaborated on several books such as *Consider the Lilies*, a devotional retelling of stories from the Bible. This collaboration is especially fitting, because Katherine credits John for having the most influence on her phenomenally successful career. During the years when she couldn't get published, he faithfully encouraged her to keep writing. Even today, when sometimes Katherine becomes discouraged and feels she can't finish a book, John will predictably tell her, "Oh, you've reached THAT stage." Just hearing those words restores Katherine's motivation and spurs her on to complete the manuscript she is working on.

Another powerful influence is novelist Flannery O'Connor, whom Katherine quotes frequently in her writing and speeches. As author Gary Schmidt points out, some of Katherine's stories "are reminiscent of Flannery O'Connor's, for in each a character is caught in a moment where the world seemingly—and sometimes not seemingly—is malevolent and threatening, where characters could easily give in to despair. And yet, suddenly, like the flash of the Christmas star, grace enters their lives, and the world that had been so desperate is full of peace and hope."[7]

Katherine adds another explanation for her interest: "Flannery O'Connor wrote what she could; I write what I can."[8]

Millions of children the world over are glad that she does.

FYInfo

Flannery O'Connor

One of Katherine Paterson's writing role models is Flannery O'Connor. Katherine believed that Flannery was able to remember what it was like to be a child and show that in her writing.

Flannery herself once said, "I was a very ancient twelve. My views at that age would have done credit to a Civil War Veteran. I'm much younger now than I was at twelve or anyway, less burdened. The weight of the centuries lies on children. I'm sure of it."[1]

Born on March 25, 1925 in Savannah, Georgia, Flannery is considered one of the greatest writers to come from the South. After attending parochial schools while she was growing up, she graduated from Georgia State College for Women (now Georgia College and State University) in 1945. Then she went on to the University of Iowa where she earned a masters degree in fine arts. A few years later she learned she had lupus. This was same autoimmune disease that had killed her father when she was only 15.

After her diagnosis, Flannery became a recluse at her mother's farm where she dedicated herself to writing for the rest of her life. She lived very quietly, seeing very few people. She died on August 3, 1964. She was only 39. During her short lifetime, she wrote two novels, more than 30 short stories and thousands of speeches and letters. Her work is remembered for its Catholic foundation and racial themes. Flannery also used symbols and metaphors throughout her narratives to bring many layers of interpretation to her writing. A collection of her short stories won the National Book Award in 1971.

Katherine wasn't the only writer to be influenced by Flannery. Flannery appears as an actual character in W.P. Kinsella's book of short stories, *Red Wolf, Red Wolf*. Kinsella also wrote the book *Shoeless Joe*, which became the basis for the famous film *Field of Dreams*.

W.P. Kinsella

CHRONOLOGY

1932 Born on October 31 in Tsing-Tsing Pu, China
1938 Leaves China and comes to the United States for a brief period
1939 Returns to China
1940 Leaves China because of the threat of war
1950 Graduates from Charles Town High School in Charles Town, Virginia
1954 Graduates from King College in Bristol, Tennessee; begins teaching in Lovettsville, Virginia
1957 Earns M.A. degree from Presbyterian School for Christian Education and leaves for Japan
1959 Begins active missionary work in Japan
1961 Returns to the United States
1962 Marries John Barstow Paterson
1963 Moves to Princeton, New Jersey; teaches sacred studies and English at Pennington School for Boys
1964 Son John is born; two-year old PoLin arrives from Hong Kong
1965 Moves to Takoma Park, Maryland
1966 Publishes *Who Am I?*; second son, David is born
1968 Adopts daughter Mary Katherine
1973 Publishes *Sign of the Chrysanthemum*
1976 Publishes *The Master Puppeteer*
1977 Publishes *Bridge to Terabithia*; wins National Book Award for *The Master Puppeteer*
1978 Publishes *The Great Gilly Hopkins*; wins Newbery Medal for *Bridge to Terabithia*
1979 Wins National Book Award and Newbery Honor for *The Great Gilly Hopkins*
1981 Wins Newbery Medal for *Jacob Have I Loved*
1986 Moves to Barre, Vermont; begins co-authoring books with her husband, John
1998 Wins Hans Christian Andersen Medal
2004 Publishes *Blueberries for the Queen*, with husband John as co-author

TIMELINE IN HISTORY

1870 Russian dictator Vladimir Lenin is born.
1887 Chinese nationalist leader Chiang Kai-shek is born.
1893 Chinese Communist Party leader Mao Zedong (also known as Mao Tse-tung) is born.
1905 Japan's victory in the Russo-Japanese War introduces it as a major world power.
1911 A revolution overthrows the Chinese imperial government and declares a republic; Sun Yat-sen is elected as the new president.
1914 World War I begins shortly after the assassination of Archduke Franz Ferdinand in the Bosnian capital of Sarajevo.
1917 Russian communists overthrown imperial Russia, making it the first country to be ruled by the Communist Party.
1918 World War I ends with the German surrender.
1921 Mao Zedong forms the Communist party in China.
1922 Hendrik Willem van Loon's *The Story of Mankind* wins the first Newbery Medal.
1925 Sun-Yat Sen dies; Chiang Kai-shek takes control of the Chinese government.
1929 The American stock market crashes, launching a worldwide depression.
1931 Japan invades Manchuria.
1933 Adolf Hitler is appointed Chancellor of Germany.
1937 Japan invades mainland China; Chinese Communists and Nationalists combine forces to fight the "Anti-Japanese War."
1939 Germany invades Poland, which begins World War II.
1941 The Japanese bomb Pearl Harbor, Hawaii, drawing the United States into World War II.
1945 The United States drops atomic bombs on two Japanese cities, killing tens of thousands; World War II ends.
1949 China becomes a Communist nation and the Nationalists withdraw to Taiwan.
1975 Chiang Kai-shek dies.
1976 Mao Zedong dies.
1991 The Soviet Union dissolves.
2004 *The Tale of Despereaux: Being the Story of a Mouse, a Princess, Some Soup, and a Spool of Thread* by Kate DiCamillo wins the Newbery Award.

FURTHER READING

For Young Adults

Adrian, Gilbert. *Going to War in World War I* (Armies of the Past). London: Franklin Watts, 2001.

Cary, Alice. *Katherine Paterson* (Meet the Author Series). Santa Barbara, California: The Learning Works, 1997.

Hansen, Ole Steen. *The War in the Trenches* (The World Wars). Austin, Texas: Raintree Steck-Vaughn, 2001.

Kite, Lorien. *The Chinese* (We Came to North America). New York: Crabtree Publishers, 2000.

Kudlinski, Kathleen V. *Pearl Harbor Is Burning!: A Story of World War II* (Once Upon America). New York: Puffin, 1993.

Malaspina, Ann. *The Chinese Revolution and Mao Zedong in World History* (In World History). Berkeley Heights, New Jersey: Enslow Publishers, 2003.

Raatma, Lucia. *Chinese Americans* (Spirit of America: Our Cultural Heritage). Chanhassen, Minnesota: Child's World, 2002.

Roberts, Russell. *John Newbery and the Story of the Newbery Medal* (Great Achievement Awards). Bear, Delaware: Mitchell Lane Publishers, 2003.

Stein, R. Conrad. *The Home Front During World War II in American History* (In American History). Berkeley Heights, New Jersey: Enslow Publishers, 2003.

Taylor, Theodore. *Air Raid -Pearl Harbor!: The Story of December 7, 1941*. New York: Harcourt, 2001.

Works Consulted

Huse, Nancy. "Katherine Paterson's Ultimate Realism." *Children's Literature Association Quarterly 9* (Fall 1984).

Jones, Linda T. "Profile: Katherine Paterson." *Language Arts,* Volume 58, Number 2, February 1981.

Paterson, Katherine. "Where Is Terabithia?" *Children's Literature Association Quarterly 9* (Winter 1984-85).

Paterson, Katherine. *Gates of Excellence: On Reading and Writing Books for Children*. New York: Dutton Children's Books, 1981.

Paterson, Katherine. "Heart in Hiding," in *Worlds of Childhood: The Art and Craft of Writing for Children*. William Zinsser (editor). Boston: Houghton Mifflin, 1990.

Paterson, Katherine. "Do I Dare Disturb the Universe?" *The Horn Book Magazine 60* (September -October 1984).

Paterson, Katherine. *The Invisible Child: On Reading and Writing Books for Children*. New York: E.P. Dutton, 2001.

Paterson, Katherine. *The Spying Heart: More Thoughts on Reading and Writing Books for Children*. New York: E.P. Dutton, 1989.

Schmidt, Gary D. *Katherine Paterson*. New York: Twayne Publishers, 1994.

On the Internet

The Official Website of Katherine Paterson
http://www.terabithia.com/
Paterson, Katherine. "I Love to Tell the Story."
http://www.ulster.net/-petersne/LOVE.pdf
Brief Biography of Pearl S. Buck
http://www.english.upenn.edu/Projects/Buck/biography.html

CHAPTER NOTES

Chapter 1
A Gate of Hope
1. Paterson, Katherine. "I Love to Tell the Story." http://www.ulster.net/-petersne/LOVE.pdf
2. Ibid.
3. Ibid.
4. Paterson, Katherine, *The Invisible Child: On Reading and Writing Books for Children*. (New York: E.P. Dutton, 2001), p. 247.
5. Ibid.
6. Ibid.
7. Ibid.
8. Paterson, Katherine. "I Love to Tell the Story." http://www.ulster.net/-petersne/LOVE.pdf

FYI: The Newbery Medal
1. The John Newbery Medal, http://www.ala.org

Chapter 2
"Spook Baby"
1. Paterson, Katherine, *The Spying Heart: More Thoughts on Reading and Writing Books for Children* (New York: E.P. Dutton, 1989), p. 51.
2. Paterson, Katherine, *Gates of Excellence: On Reading and Writing Books for Children* (New York: Dutton Children's Books, 1981), p. 103.

Chapter 3
A Lonely Heart
1. Jones, Linda T, "Profile: Katherine Paterson." (*Language Arts,* Volume 58, Number 2, February 1981), p. 195.
2. Paterson, Katherine, *Gates of Excellence: On Reading and Writing Books for Children* (New York: Dutton Children's Books, 1981), p. 100.
3. Schmidt, Gary D., *Katherine Paterson* (New York: Twayne Publishers, 1994), p. 6.
4. Jones, Linda T, "Profile: Katherine Paterson." (*Language Arts,* Volume 58, Number 2, February 1981), p. 195.
5. Paterson, Katherine, *The Invisible Child: On Reading and Writing Books for Children* (New York: E.P. Dutton, 2001), p. 134.
6. Ibid., p. 178.

Chapter 4
The Writer Emerges
1. Jones, Linda T, "Profile: Katherine Paterson." (*Language Arts,* Volume 58, Number 2, February 1981), p. 191.
2. Paterson, Katherine, *The Spying Heart: More Thoughts on Reading and Writing Books for Children* (New York: E.P. Dutton, 1989), p. 53.
3. Paterson, Katherine, *Gates of Excellence: On Reading and Writing Books for Children* (New York: Dutton Children's Books, 1981), p. 8.
4. Jones, Linda T, "Profile: Katherine Paterson." (*Language Arts,* Volume 58, Number 2, February 1981), p. 191.

CHAPTER NOTES CONT'D

5. Paterson, Katherine, *Gates of Excellence: On Reading and Writing Books for Children* (New York: Dutton Children's Books, 1981), p. 83.

Chapter 5
An Honored Author

1. Terabithia.com – Katherine Paterson – Questions; http://www.terabithia.com/questions.html
2. Paterson, Katherine, *The Invisible Child: On Reading and Writing Books for Children.* (New York: E.P. Dutton, 2001), p. 48.
3. Ibid., p. 175.
4. Paterson, Katherine, *Gates of Excellence: On Reading and Writing Books for Children* (New York: Dutton Children's Books, 1981), p. 139.
5. Jones, Linda T, "Profile: Katherine Paterson." (*Language Arts,* Volume 58, Number 2, February 1981), p. 194.
6. *The Invisible Child*, p. 74.
7. Schmidt, Gary D., *Katherine Paterson* (New York: Twayne Publishers, 1994), p. 69.
8. Paterson, Katherine, *Gates of Excellence: On Reading and Writing Books for Children* (New York: Dutton Children's Books, 1981), p. 37.

FYI: Flannery O'Conner

1. Paterson, Katherine, *Gates of Excellence: On Reading and Writing Books for Children* (New York: Dutton Children's Books, 1981), p. 50.

GLOSSARY

Bunraku (byun-RAW-koo)
A traditional Japanese puppet theater featuring large puppets operated by onstage puppeteers with the story narrated from offstage.

diorama (die-uh-RAM-uh)
picture that includes realistic characters and details with a scenic background.

feudal (FEW-dull)
an historical period in which nobles controlled the land and the people living on it; most of these people were farmers who gave the nobles a portion of their crops in exchange for protection.

malevolent (muh-LEV-uh-lent)
intending or producing an evil outcome.

mimic (MIH-mick)
a person who imitates other people.

recluse (REH-cloose)
someone who lives almost entirely by himself or herself.

shrapnel (SHRAP-null)
sharp, jagged fragments from a bursting shell.

INDEX

Bridge to Terabithia 10, 28, 37, 39
Buck, Pearl 35
Chiang Kai-shek 13
Consider the Lilies 41
Cry, the Beloved Country 23
Great Gilly Hopkins, The 37, 40
Hill, Lisa 8, 9
Hitler, Adolf 16, 25
Hopkins, Gerard Manley 27
Japan 15, 16, 17
Jacob Have I Loved 37
Jiangsu, China 13
Kinsella, W.P. 42
Manchuria 15, 17
Mao Zedong 13
Master Puppeteer, The 33
Newbery, John 11
Newbery Honor Book 37
Newbery Medal 10, 11, 37
O'Connor, Flannery 41, 42
Of Nightingales That Weep 33
Paterson, David, (son) 7, 31
Paterson, Elizabeth PoLin (daughter)
 .... 31, 32. 34
Paterson, John (son) 31
Paterson, Mary Katherine (daughter)
 31
Paterson, John Barstow (husband) ....
 .... 30, 40, 41
Paterson, Katherine
   Awards 34, 38, 39

Beginnings as a writer 32
Cancer 8-9
College years 24, 27
Criticism of work 39
Childhood 23
Feelings about writing, ... 40
High school 24
Marriage 30
Missionary in Japan 29
Years as a teacher 27-28
Pearl Harbor 21, 25
Peck, Richard 37
Presbyterian Mission Board 16, 23
Shanghai 20
Shanghai American 20
Sign of the Chrysanthemum 32, 38
Spencer, Nancy 21
Who Am I? 31
Womeldorf, Ann, (sister) 14
Womeldorf, George Raymond
   (father) 13, 14, 16
Womeldorf, Mary Goetchius
   (mother) 13, 14
Womeldorf, Helen, (sister) 14
Womeldorf, Raymond (Sonny)
   (brother) 14 23
Womeldorf, Lizzie (sister) 23
World War II 21, 23, 25